William Shakespeare
The
Tempest

First published 2015 by Walker Books Ltd
87 Vauxhall Walk, London SE11 5HJ

2 4 6 8 10 9 7 5 3 1

© 1998, 2014, 2015 Marcia Williams

The right of Marcia Williams to be identified as author/illustrator of this work
has been asserted by her in accordance with the Copyright, Designs and Patents Act 1988

This book has been typeset in Kennerly Regular

Printed and bound in China

British Library Cataloguing in Publication Data:
a catalogue record for this book is available from the British Library

ISBN 978-1-4063-6273-2

www.walker.co.uk

William Shakespeare
The Tempest

Retold by
Marcia Williams

Contents

In which Miranda
learns the truth.

Many years ago, off the shore of a small, mystical isle, a ship struggled in the eye of a terrible tempest. The thunder roared, the lightning cracked and the waves raised the ship up towards the stormy clouds. There it seemed to rest for a moment, only to be dashed down into the brink by the raging sea. No ship could survive such a battering. No sailor could survive in such waters.

From the island, Miranda, a young and
very beautiful girl, watched in horror as
the ship fought to survive and the sailors
cried out in fear. Sitting beside Miranda
was her loving father, Prospero, his cloak
flapping in the wind and his great staff
held out towards the storm. He had been
preparing for this moment for years. From
his cell-like dwelling on the island, Prospero
had been developing his magic powers from

a rare book. Now his skill was so great that he could even control the elements.

Miranda suspected that her father had caused the storm, but had no idea why such a gentle man should wish to harm anyone. "If by your art, my dearest father, you have put the wild waters in this roar, allay them," she pleaded, clutching at his arm.

"Be collected," replied her father. "No more amazement. Tell your piteous heart there's no harm done. 'Tis time I should inform thee farther. Lend thy hand and pluck my magic garment from me."

Prospero laid his cloak and great staff beside him and took his daughter's hands in his. "Canst thou remember a time before we came unto this cell?" he asked. "I do not think thou canst, for then thou wast not out three years old."

Bit by bit, Prospero revealed how he and Miranda had been cast away on the island, twelve years before. In those days, Prospero had been Duke of Milan, but he was always in his library studying his books, and he left

most of his duties to his brother Antonio.
Eventually Antonio decided that if he was
to do all the work, he should have Prospero's
title as well! Aided by Alonso, King of
Naples, he set about seizing the dukedom
and getting rid of his brother. Prospero was
very popular with the people of Milan, so
Antonio and King Alonso did not dare kill
him outright. Instead, they set him and his
little daughter, Miranda, adrift in a tiny
boat. Luckily Prospero's friend Gonzalo had

secreted some clothes and other provisions on board, as well as Prospero's most precious books. These sustained the duke and his daughter until, after many long nights and days, they drifted to their island.

"Dost thou attend me?" Prospero asked his Miranda as their history unfolded.

"Your tale, sir, would cure deafness," she replied in wonder.

In which Miranda and
Prince Ferdinand meet.

Before Miranda and Prospero arrived
on the island, the only inhabitants were
Caliban, a monster, and some sprites which
Caliban's mother, a foul witch, had trapped
in trees before she died. Caliban, a strange

and unearthly creature, became Prospero's
servant, as did Ariel, an airy little sprite
who was invisible to all but Prospero. Ariel
had been freed from a tree by Prospero's
magic and in return had promised to serve
him faithfully for twelve years.

Because Miranda had lived nearly all
her life on the island, she could not really
remember ever seeing another human apart
from her father. Now, Prospero told her, she
was about to see that not all humans were
as grey and aged as him; for, along with the
sailors, the storm-tossed ship had brought

his friend Gonzalo, his enemies Antonio
and King Alonso, and the king's son Prince
Ferdinand to the island.

As Prospero was telling Miranda this,
Ariel approached. Prospero put his magic
cloak back on and, with a wave of his staff,
he sent Miranda to sleep.

"Approach, my Ariel; come!" he called.

"All hail, great master, grave sir, hail! I
come to answer thy best pleasure," replied
the sprite.

Ariel was triumphant, for he had managed
to rescue all those aboard the ship. He had

brought the vessel safely into a hidden inlet and spirited everyone ashore, isolating all but Antonio, Gonzalo and King Alonso. Thanks to Ariel and Prospero's ingenuity, Prince Ferdinand thought his father must have drowned. Indeed, each thought he was the only survivor of the tempest.

"But are they, Ariel, safe?" pressed Prospero, who had no desire to cause lasting harm.

"Not a hair perish'd," Ariel reassured him with pride.

Prospero smiled. He was pleased with the sprite, but told him there was still more work to be done.

"Is there more toil?" grumbled Ariel.

"How now? Moody?" admonished

Prospero sharply. "Dost thou forget from what a torment I did free thee?"

"No," sulked the sprite.

"If thou more murmur'st, I will rend an oak and peg thee in his knotty entrails till thou has howl'd away twelve winters!" threatened Prospero.

This was enough to make Ariel hang upon Prospero's every word! Off he went as ordered, in the guise of a sea nymph, to bring the young Prince Ferdinand to Prospero's cave.

Prospero then called upon Caliban to go and gather wood.

"There's wood enough within," grumbled Caliban.

"Hag-seed, hence!" snapped Prospero. "Fetch us in fuel; and be quick."

"I must obey: his art is of such power," said Caliban, who secretly longed for every toad, beetle and bat to land on his master.

Moments later, Ferdinand was drawn towards Prospero's cave by Ariel's singing. Miranda woke to a sight so new to her that she could only stare in wonder and delight.

"It carries a brave form: but 'tis a spirit," she murmured.

"No, wench," smiled her father. "It eats and sleeps, and hath such senses as we have."

"I might call him a thing divine," she said, and her heart missed several beats!

Then Ferdinand saw Miranda and his heart also missed several beats! He had seen many fair faces, but never had he seen one to compare with Miranda's.

"O you wonder!" he gasped. "My prime request is if you be maid or no?"

"No wonder, sir," smiled Miranda, "but certainly a maid."

So it was that these two youngsters fell in love at this first meeting, just as Prospero had planned. Yet Prospero, thinking that love so easily and quickly come by might not last, decided to throw a few problems in their path. Adversity, he hoped, would seal their lovers' bond. With this aim, he accused Ferdinand of spying.

"Thou hast put thyself upon this island as a spy, to win it from me, the Lord on't," he charged Ferdinand.

"No, as I am a man," protested Ferdinand.

"There's nothing ill can dwell in such a temple," cried Miranda, devastated at her father's angry tone.

"Speak not you for him," snapped Prospero. "He's a traitor! Come, I'll manacle thy neck and feet together."

Prospero forbade Miranda to talk to Ferdinand, and set him to shift logs. Being a prince, Ferdinand was not used to such labour, but he did it willingly to stay close to his new love.

Ferdinand hauled logs for hours, but as soon as Prospero's back was turned, Miranda went to offer him her help. "I'll bear your logs the while," she said.

"No, precious creature," puffed Ferdinand.

"I had rather crack my sinews, break my back, than you should such dishonour undergo."

Ferdinand continued to move the logs and Miranda continued to distract him with her presence, so that each log took longer and longer to haul. The pair were so absorbed in each other that they failed to notice Prospero, who was hidden nearby, watching their love blossom. When he had seen enough to reassure himself of Ferdinand's good intentions, he appeared

suddenly, making them both jump. Miranda
expected to be admonished for disobeying
her father's orders and keeping company
with Ferdinand, but Prospero smiled and
turned to Ferdinand. "If I have too austerely
punish'd you, your compensation makes
amends – take my daughter," he said.

He then conjured up a flock of nymphs
to sing a blessing on their engagement, and
told them to rest and talk together all they
liked, for he had work to do. Miranda and
Ferdinand were delighted.

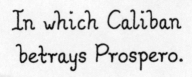

In which Caliban
betrays Prospero.

Meanwhile, down by the shore, Caliban
was gathering driftwood, grumbling about
Prospero all the while. "All the infections
that the sun sucks up from bogs, fens, flats,
on Prospero fall," he snarled.

Yet Caliban was terrified of Prospero's
magic powers, and when a figure came along
the beach, he was convinced that it was one
of Prospero's sprites come to torment him.

He hurriedly threw himself to the ground and hid under his cloak. "Lo now! Lo!" he cried in panic. "I'll fall flat."

However, the figure was no sprite – it was Trinculo, King Alonso's jester, who was wandering around the isle looking for other survivors of the shipwreck. He spied the cloak upon the ground with hideous limbs protruding from it at odd angles.

"What have we here?" he pondered. "A man or a fish? Dead or alive? A fish, he smells like a fish, a strange fish!"

Suddenly there was a crack of thunder. Trinculo feared another storm was coming and looked about for shelter. There was none – except Caliban's cloak. Trinculo forced himself to ignore the smell and the strange limbs and crawl under the stinking, ragged pile. "Misery acquaints a man with strange bedfellows," he cried.

Minutes later, Stefano, the king's drunken butler, fell over the heaving bundle. "This is some monster of the isle!" he cried in fright when Caliban poked his head out. Then

Trinculo appeared and Stefano clapped his hands in delight. A friend from the ship at last, and one he could share a drink with!

Caliban, who was unaware of the shipwreck and who had never seen any humans apart from Prospero and Miranda, decided Trinculo and Stefano must be gods. "Hast thou not dropped from heaven?" he enquired.

"Out o' the moon, I do assure thee: I was the man in the moon, when time was," teased the drunken Stefano.

Caliban was as stupid as he was ugly and

believed that, having come from the moon, they must be very powerful. He promised the pair that they would have the island for themselves and him as their slave, if only they would assassinate Prospero. "Thou shalt be lord of it," Caliban told Stefano eagerly.

It did not take much to persuade Stefano that being a king would be more fun than being a servant to a king, so he readily agreed. "Monster, I will kill this man," he declared, as though murder was no more trouble than taking another swig from his bottle of wine.

Ariel, who was hovering unseen above their drunken heads, overheard every word they said, and flew off to tell his master. So when the traitor Caliban and his companions drew near Prospero's cave, Prospero was ready. Ariel had scattered Prospero's finest

clothes in front of the cave, on the magician's order. Then he and Prospero made themselves invisible and watched.

Caliban, Trinculo and Stefano crept rather noisily towards the cave, ready to kill Prospero. "Pray you, tread softly, that the blind mole may not hear a foot fall: we now are near his cell," whispered Caliban.

Just then, his foolish companions saw
that they were treading on garments
richly embroidered with gold and pearls
– garments fit for a king. For a moment all
thoughts of assassination left them.

"O King Stefano! Look what a wardrobe
here is for thee!" cried out Trinculo.

"Put off that gown, Trinculo; by this
hand, I'll have that gown," returned Stefano.

In no time at all, the drunken pair were
dancing about, half-dressed in the courtly

clothes, while Caliban pleaded with them to murder Prospero before they were all discovered and turned into barnacles. When Prospero saw that they were completely distracted, he unleashed his punishment: a pack of snarling phantom hounds. "Hey Mountain, hey! Fury, Fury! There, Tyrant, there! Hark, hark!" shouted Prospero, waving his magic staff.

"Hark, they roar!" laughed Ariel.

"Let them be hunted soundly," ordered Prospero.

Ariel drove the dogs forward, and the terrified rascals ran before them. The trio were chased far off across the island until they collapsed into a pathetic heap, all breath and ambition worn out of them. Ariel dismissed the phantom hounds and returned to Prospero, another job well done.

In which Prospero prepares his tormentors for a fall.

The time had come for the most important part of Prospero's plan: to settle the score with his brother and King Alonso. After the shipwreck, when King Alonso, Antonio and the good Gonzalo had unravelled themselves from the seaweed and wiped the sea salt from their eyes, they found, to their amazement, that they were quite unhurt. Their only distress was that the king's son, Ferdinand, who had been the first to throw himself out of the lurching ship, was not with them. They immediately set out in search of him. For hours they had desperately combed the beaches, but they found no sign of Prince Ferdinand or any other survivors.

"He is drowned whom thus we stray to find," cried King Alonso, "and the sea mocks our frustrate search on land."

Gonzalo feared that the king was right and that the young prince had drowned, but he did not say so. "By your patience," he said instead, "I needs must rest me."

They were all tired, hungry and in despair, so the king consented to the old man's request. As the men dropped to the sand, they heard enchanting music. Strange beings materialized as if from nowhere, carrying a wonderful, richly scented feast.

This they lay in front of the weary men, before vanishing as mysteriously as they had arrived. Prospero, cloaked in invisibility, stood by and watched.

"What were these?" wondered King Alonso – although hunger made him more eager to eat than think. "I will stand to and feed," he announced, deciding a throne might be more than he should expect.

Just as the three men were about to tuck into the delicious banquet, there was a rushing of wind and a clap of thunder and lightning. Ariel, disguised as a harpy, flapped his wings upon the table and the food vanished! "You fools!" he cried, and

then, in shocking detail, he reminded them of their sins against Prospero and his innocent child.

Guilt and fear froze their spirits:

everything the harpy accused them of was
true. Their sins began to weigh heavily on
them. Then Ariel, invisible once again, drew
the unhappy nobles closer to Prospero's cell.
There he led them into a magic circle formed
by Prospero, which held them like unwilling
statues. Delighted, Prospero sent Ariel to
fetch his old sword, hat and duke's robes.

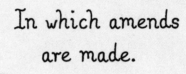

In which amends
are made.

When Ariel had helped Prospero into this attire, Prospero smiled. "Why, that's my dainty Ariel! I shall miss thee," he said. "But yet thou shall have freedom."

Then he appeared before his brother and King Alonso dressed just as he would have been twelve years before. To their guilty minds, it appeared that Prospero had risen from the dead.

"Behold, Sir King, the wronged Duke of Milan," Prospero announced.

Even Gonzalo, who was innocent of all wrongdoing, gasped at this vision from their past. Could he be real, or would he vanish as strangely as he had appeared, like the phantom feast? When Prospero did not vanish and they realized that he was truly the old duke, Antonio and King Alonso were awestruck into true repentance. They begged to be forgiven.

"Thy dukedom I resign, and do entreat thou

pardon me my wrongs," pleaded King Alonso.

Prospero ignored him for a moment as he went to embrace his noble friend, Gonzalo, who had behaved with such honour. Then, since King Alonso and Antonio were truly repentant, Prospero's anger was finally placated.

"My dukedom since you have given me again, I will requite you with as good a thing," he said to King Alonso.

Prospero released the three men from the circle and led them to where Ferdinand and Miranda sat playing chess.

King Alonso hardly dared to believe his eyes. "If this prove a vision of the island, one dear son shall I twice lose," he said, shaking his head in disbelief.

Ferdinand jumped up and ran to kneel at his father's feet. "Though the seas threaten, they are merciful: I have curs'd them without cause," he cried in relief.

King Alonso touched his son's head and, finding he was not a vision of his imagination, raised him from the ground and embraced him warmly.

"What is this maid, with whom thou wast at play?" he enquired. "Is she the goddess that hath sever'd us?"

"Sir, she is mortal," smiled Ferdinand, "but by immortal Providence she's mine."

Ferdinand
then told
King Alonso
that he

wished to marry Miranda. "I chose her when
I could not ask my father," he explained.

Seeing Miranda's beauty and his son's
happiness, the king gave his consent. Like
Prospero, he hoped the union would heal the
rift between Milan and Naples. "Let grief
and sorrow still embrace his heart that doth
not wish you joy!" he cried.

"Be it so," said old Gonzalo warmly.
"Amen!"

Into the midst of their rejoicing, Caliban,
Trinculo and Stefano arrived, urged on by
Ariel. They were still a little the worse for

drink, still in their stolen apparel, and still moving slowly and with great difficulty.

"I have been in such a pickle," moaned Trinculo.

"I am not Stefano, but a cramp," groaned Stefano.

"I shall be pinch'd to death," grumbled Caliban.

It would be true to say that no one felt sorry for the strange looking trio. Strangest of all was Caliban, for none of the nobles had ever seen his like before. Now that his dukedom had been restored, Prospero was

of a mind to forgive these would-be assassins
too, but only in return for a little hard labour.

"Go, sirrah, to my cell," he ordered Caliban.
"Take with you your companions: as you look
to have my pardon, trim it handsomely."

So they did, for even Caliban had grown
a little wiser and would not risk upsetting
Prospero again.

The rest of the party then made themselves
comfortable, while Prospero entertained
them with tales of his and Miranda's
adventures over the past twelve years.

The following morning they all planned to
sail to Naples to celebrate the wedding of
Miranda and Ferdinand. The happy couple,
as everyone noted, were still quite unable to
take their eyes off each other, and were not in
the least interested in Prospero's storytelling!
Prospero looked forward to returning to
Milan as its rightful duke after the wedding;
a duke who would now pay more attention to
his duties than his library.

In which Ariel is freed.

Later that night, while everyone slept, Prospero released his faithful Ariel. No longer would Ariel have to obey his commands, but could fly as free as any sprite might wish. In return, Ariel promised him fair winds and calm seas for the journey home. Then Prospero discarded his magic cloak, buried his staff deep in the ground and threw his book of magic out to sea.

After twelve years, Prospero was leaving the enchanted island to Caliban and the sprites. Prospero's tempest had served its purpose, and his dukedom was restored. He had no further use for magic. "Now my charms are all o'erthrown, and what strength I have's mine own," he whispered to the watching eyes of the night.

WILLIAM SHAKESPEARE was a popular playwright, poet and actor who lived in Elizabethan England. He married in Stratford-upon-Avon aged eighteen and had three children, although one died in childhood. Shakespeare then moved to London, where he wrote 39 plays and over 150 sonnets, many of which are still very popular today. In fact, his plays are performed more often than those of any other playwright, and he died 450 years ago! His gravestone includes a curse against interfering with his burial place, possibly to deter people from opening it in search of unpublished manuscripts. It reads, "Blessed be the man that spares these stones, and cursed be he that moves my bones." Spooky!

MARCIA WILLIAMS' mother was a novelist and her father a playwright, so it's not surprising that Marcia ended up an author herself. Although she never trained formally as an artist, she found that motherhood, and the time she spent later as a nursery school teacher, inspired her to start writing and illustrating children's books.

Marcia's books bring to life some of the world's all-time favourite stories and some colourful historical characters. Her hilarious retellings and clever observations will have children laughing out loud and coming back for more!